Samuel French Acting Edition

Uncle Vanya

by Anton Chekhov
a new version by Annie Baker

based on a literal translation by
Margarita Shalina

SAMUELFRENCH.COM   SAMUELFRENCH.CO.UK

FOR PRODUCTION ENQUIRIES

UNITED STATES AND CANADA
Info@SamuelFrench.com
1-866-598-8449

UNITED KINGDOM AND EUROPE
Plays@SamuelFrench.co.uk
020-7255-4302

Each title is subject to availability from Samuel French, depending upon country of performance. Please be aware that UNCLE VANYA may not be licensed by Samuel French in your territory. Professional and amateur producers should contact the nearest Samuel French office or licensing partner to verify availability.

MUSIC USE NOTE

Licensees are solely responsible for obtaining formal written permission from copyright owners to use copyrighted music in the performance of this play and are strongly cautioned to do so. If no such permission is obtained by the licensee, then the licensee must use only original music that the licensee owns and controls. Licensees are solely responsible and liable for all music clearances and shall indemnify the copyright owners of the play(s) and their licensing agent, Samuel French, against any costs, expenses, losses and liabilities arising from the use of music by licensees. Please contact the appropriate music licensing authority in your territory for the rights to any incidental music.

IMPORTANT BILLING AND CREDIT REQUIREMENTS

If you have obtained performance rights to this title, please refer to your licensing agreement for important billing and credit requirements.

UNCLE VANYA had its world premiere at SoHo Rep in New York City on June 7, 2012 (Sarah Benson, Artistic Director; Tania Camargo, Executive Director). The performance was directed by Sam Gold, with sets by Andrew Lieberman, costumes by Annie Baker, lighting by Mark Barton, sound by Matt Tierney, and props by Kate Foster. The Production Stage Manager was Christina Lowe. The cast was as follows:

VANYA	Reed Birney
YELENA	Maria Dizzia
MARINA	Georgia Engel
THE PROFESSOR	Peter Friedman
WAFFLES	Matthew Maher
MARIA	Rebecca Schull
ASTROV	Michael Shannon
YEFIM	Paul Thureen
SONYA	Merritt Wever

CHARACTERS

VOINITSKY, Ivan Petrovich (Vanya), Maria Vasilyevna's son

YELENA ANDREYEVNA, the professor's wife, twenty-seven years old

MARINA, an old nanny

SEREBRYAKOV, Alexander Vladimirovich, a retired professor

TELEGIN, Ilya Ilyich, an impoverished landowner

VOINITSKAYA, Maria Vasilyevna, widow of a privy councillor, mother of the professor's first wife

ASTROV, Mikhail Lvovich, a doctor

YEFIM (Hired Man/Night Watchman)

SOPHIA ALEXANDROVNA (Sonya),the professor's daughter from his first marriage

SETTING

The action takes place on Serebryakov's estate.

TIME

Present Day

AUTHOR'S NOTES

What follows could be called a translation or an adaptation, depending on how you define the terms. I worked initially with a literal translation commissioned specifically for this project, and then, in my final draft, with the original Russian text. Very little has been "updated"; no cultural references have been changed or omitted. In fact, a particular goal of this translation/adaptation was to preserve all the quoting and name-dropping that takes place in the original Russian. (Waffles's exclamation "It was a scene worthy of Aivazovsky!" is usually translated as "It was a scene worthy of a painter of shipwrecks!"). Similarly, the grammar of the original text – endless run-on sentences, ellipses, the awkward repetition of words – has been paid special attention. Words like "creep" are an attempt to loyally translate the slang of 19th Century Russia.

The goal was to create a version that would make Chekhov happy; to create a version that sounds to our contemporary American ears the way the play sounded to Russian ears during the play's first productions in the provinces in 1898. We will never know if that goal was achieved, but it was the guiding principle behind this text.

– Annie Baker
New York City, July 2012

ACT ONE

(A garden. A section of the house is visible, along with the verandah. A table set for tea underneath an old poplar. Benches, chairs. A guitar lies on one of the benches. Not far from the table is a swing. It's between 2 and 3 in the afternoon. Overcast.)

*(**MARINA**, a sedentary old woman, sits by the samovar, knitting a stocking. **ASTROV** walks around nearby.)*

MARINA. *(pouring a cup of tea)* You should eat something.

ASTROV. *(reluctantly taking the cup)* I don't feel like it.

MARINA. How 'bout a little vodka?

ASTROV. No.

I don't *always* drink vodka, you know.

It's too hot anyway.

(Pause.)

ASTROV. Nanny, how long have we known each other?

MARINA. *(thinking it over)* How long? God help me. Hmmm. Let's see…you first came here…when? Sonyechka's mother was still alive…Vera Petrovna…you stayed with us twice, two different winters…so…eleven years?

(after a moment)

Maybe more.

ASTROV. Have I changed?

MARINA. Oh yes. You were young then, very handsome, and now you're old. You're not as attractive anymore.

You also drink.

ASTROV. Yep. In ten years I've turned into a completely different person. You wanna know why? I work too much, Nanny. I'm on my feet all day, I never relax, and then at night I lie awake in bed, just waiting for someone to come knock on my door and drag me away to see another patient. I haven't had one day off the entire time you've known me. Of course I seem old.

Yeah, and for what it is, life is pretty boring and stupid. You're surrounded by creeps, you spend all day hanging out with creeps, a few years go by and little by little, without even realizing it, you become a creep yourself. It's unavoidable.

(he twirls his moustache)

Yeesh, and I've grown this huge moustache. It looks stupid, doesn't it?

I've become a creep, Nanny.

Although, you know, I'm not a complete idiot. My brain still works, thank god. But I feel sorta numb. I don't want anything, I don't need anything, I don't love anybody...well, you. I love you.

(he kisses her on the head)

I had a Nanny just like you when I was a boy.

MARINA. You should eat something.

ASTROV. No.

I was in Malitskoe during Lent...for the epidemic... typhus...and the peasants were lying side by side in these little cabins, almost on top of each other...I mean, the filth, the stench, the air was filled with smoke, cows were lying on the floor right next to people...pigs, too...I worked all day, I didn't sit down once, didn't eat or drink, and when I finally get home they don't let me go to sleep...there's been an accident...they bring me this switchman from the railroad, I put him on the table so I can operate...and then he up and dies on me under chloroform.

And just when I didn't need it, these emotions started flooding in, and...this...this thought just kind of *nipped* at my conscience...

The thought that maybe, just maybe, I had intentionally killed him.

(pause)

I sat down—I closed my eyes—like this—and I thought: those who live one or two hundred years after us, the people for whom we—we—we clear the road, will they say nice things about us? Nanny, they won't even remember!

MARINA. People won't remember, but God will.

ASTROV. Ha. Thank you. Well said.

(Enter VOINITSKY *from the house. He has just taken a nap and he has a crumpled look to him. He takes a seat on a bench and adjusts his dandyish necktie.)*

VOINITSKY. Yep.

(Pause.)

VOINITSKY. ...Yes.

ASTROV. Sleep well?

VOINITSKY. Oh yes, very.

(He yawns.)

VOINITSKY. Ever since the professor moved here with his, uh...

(he wipes the sleep from his eyes)

...spouse, things have gone totally haywire. I sleep during the day, I eat Caucasian stews, I drink wine... it's not healthy. I never used to have free time...Sonya and I were always working...now she does everything herself. And I sleep and eat and drink.

Not. Good.

MARINA. *(shaking her head)* The samovar has been on all morning, but the professor gets up at noon. We used to have lunch at one, like normal people...now we eat at six or seven. Then at night the professor wants to read and write, but at two am he's calling for me... "What is it, sweetie?" Tea, Nanny! Wake everyone up, put on the samovar!

What a way to live.

ASTROV. How long are they staying?

VOINITSKY. *(whistles)* A hundred years. The professor wants to settle down here.

MARINA. It's the same thing today. The samovar's been on the table for two hours, and they've gone for a walk.

VOINITSKY. They're coming, they're coming...act normal.

(Voices are heard from the garden—they are returning from their walk...enter SEREBRYAKOV, YELENA ANDREYEVNA, SONYA *and* TELEGIN.*)*

SEREBRYAKOV. Very nice, very nice. Wonderful views.

TELEGIN. Remarkable, Your Excellency.

SONYA. We're going to the forest tomorrow, Papa. Do you want to come?

VANYA. *(pointedly)* Tea time, ladies and gentleman!

SEREBRYAKOV. Friends—would you be willing to send the tea to my study? I still have a little more work to do today, I just have to...

(He trails off and starts to exit.)

SONYA. I think you'd really like it...

*(*YELENA, SEREBRYAKOV, *and* SONYA *enter the house;* TELEGIN *goes up to the table and sits down beside* MARINA.*)*

VOINITSKY. It's hot outside, it's disgusting, and our famous scholar is in a coat and galoshes, holding an umbrella and wearing gloves.

ASTROV. He's trying to take care of himself.

VOINITSKY. *(re:* YELENA*)* God, she's good-looking.

TELEGIN. You know, Marina Timofeyevna, I was thinking. Whether I'm riding my horse through a field, or taking a walk in the shady garden...or even now, just sitting here, looking at this table in front of me...I am capable of experiencing extreme bliss!

The weather's wonderful, the birds are singing, we live in peace and harmony...I mean, what more could you ask for?

(accepting a glass)

I am grateful!

VOINITSKY. *(lost in thought)* Her eyes. Jesus. Amazing woman.

ASTROV. Tell us about something else, Ivan Petrovich. Talk to us.

VOINITSKY. *(listlessly)* What do you want me to talk about?

ASTROV. There's nothing new?

VOINITSKY. Nope. Nothing. I'm the same as always. Actually, I'm worse. I'm lazy and I don't do anything and I'm whiny and bitter. Like a piece of horseradish. Oh, and *maman*, that old crow, she's still going on and on about women's liberation.

ASTROV. And the professor?

VOINITSKY. And the professor sits in his study all day and writes.

How does it go?

"With tired minds and furrowed brows/We write ode after ode/Not for ourselves/And not for the praise we'll never hear."

I feel bad for the paper.

He should be writing his autobiography instead. That's a good story. You see, our retired professor is an old bread crust, a, uh...a dried-up fish. He has gout. Rheumatism. Migraines. His liver is inflamed with envy and regret. And now he lives here—thanks to his first wife—because he can't afford to live in the city anymore. Oh, and he's always complaining about his misfortune, even though he's unbelievably lucky.

(agitated)

I mean, think about how lucky he is! The son of a sexton, a seminary student, he's managed to get all these academic degrees and professorships...people call him "Your Excellency"...he's son-in-law to a senator...Not that any of this is important, by the way. But think about it: here's a person who has been reading and writing about art for twenty-five years, and he understands *absolutely nothing* about it! For twenty five years he's been rehashing other people's thoughts about realism, naturalism, blahblahblah, for twenty five years he's been writing things that intelligent people already know and stupid people aren't even interested in...that's twenty-five years just...emptied into the void. And what egotism! He's so pretentious! Now he's retired, nobody's ever heard of him, he's a total unknown, which means that for twenty-five years he's used up...

(he trails off)

And he walks around like he's some kind of demigod!

ASTROV. So you're jealous of him.

VOINITSKY. Of course I'm jealous! And his success with women! He's like Don Juan! His first wife—my sister—a beautiful, gentle creature, pure as this blue sky, honest, kind, I mean she had more suitors than he's had students—she loved him, really loved him, the way only angels can love...my mother, his mother-in-law, she still adores him, she's *obsessed* with him. His second wife, beautiful, smart—you saw her just now—she married him when he was already an old man. She gave her youth to him, her beauty, her...her freedom. I mean, what for? Why?

ASTROV. Is she faithful?

VOINITSKY. Uh, yes. Unfortunately.

ASTROV. Why is it unfortunate?

VOINITSKY. Because her fidelity is false. It's good rhetoric but it's bad logic. To marry an old man, a man you

can't stand, that's immoral, but then to silence your
youth and your desires and your spirit in order to stay
with him...that's *not* immoral? That's a good thing?

TELEGIN. *(near tears)* Vanya, I don't like it when you talk like
this. Being unfaithful to your wife or your husband,
that's...that's...that's...that's like being unfaithful to
your country!

VOINITSKY. Oh, shut up, Waffles.

TELEGIN. Allow me, Vanya. My wife ran away the day after
our wedding with another man on account of my...
uh...my unbecoming exterior. But I take my duty
seriously. I still love her and I'm faithful to her...I help
her out whenever I can...I gave her my property so she
could stay there and raise the children she had with
this other man. I'm not happy, I lost my happiness
long ago, but I still have my pride. And her? She's
getting older, her beauty has faded—in keeping with
the laws of nature—and the man she loved has died.

So what does she have left?

(Enter SONYA *and* YELENA; *not long after* MARIA
VASILYEVNA *enters with a book. She sits and reads, she
is given tea, and she drinks without looking up.)*

SONYA. *(hurriedly, to* MARINA*)* Nannechka, the peasants are
here. Go talk to them, and I'll do the tea...

*(*SONYA *pours the tea.* MARINA *exits.* YELENA
ANDREYEVNA *takes her cup and drinks, sitting on the
swing. Silence for a while.)*

ASTROV. *(to* YELENA*)* I came to see your husband. You wrote
me that he was sick, rheumatism and something else,
but he seems perfectly healthy.

YELENA. Well, last night he was moping around and
complaining about the pain in his legs. Today, nothing.

ASTROV. While I rode thirty versts and almost broke my
neck getting here. Ah well. It's fine, it's not the first
time. I'll stay here tonight and then at least I can have
my sleep *quantum satis.*

SONYA. Oh, good! You never spend the night. Have you eaten?

ASTROV. No ma'am.

SONYA. Then you're eating with us. We have lunch between six and seven now.

(She drinks.)

SONYA. The tea is cold.

TELEGIN. The, uh, temperature of the samovar has dropped considerably.

YELENA. It's fine, Ivan Ivanich, we'll drink it cold.

TELEGIN. Uh...miss...I'm so sorry to...but my name is not Ivan Ivanich. It's Ilya Ilyich. Ilya Ilyich Telegin. Or, as some call me on account of my pockmarked face, Waffles. I've known Sonyechka since she was a baby, I helped baptize her, and your husband, uh, His Excellency, he knows me very well. I live here now. I live with you. If you'd be kind enough to notice, I, uh, I eat meals with you every day.

SONYA. Ilya Ilyich is our right-hand man.

(tenderly)

Pass me your cup, Godfather. I'll pour you some more tea.

MARIA VASILYEVNA. Akh!

SONYA. What's wrong, Babushka?

MARIA VASILYEVNA. I forgot to tell Alexander...my memory is terrible...I got a letter today from Kharkov. Pavel Alekseyevich sent a new pamphlet.

ASTROV. Is it interesting?

MARIA VASILYEVNA. Interesting, yes, but very strange...he's refuting the same idea he upheld seven years ago. I think it's terrible.

VOINITSKY. There's nothing terrible about it. Drink your tea, *maman.*

MARIA VASILYEVNA. I want to talk about it! Why can't I talk about it?

VOINITSKY. We've been talking and talking and reading pamphlets for fifty years. Maybe it's time we end it.

MARIA VASILYEVNA. You just don't like the sound of my voice anymore. You find me unpleasant for some reason. I'm sorry, *Jean*, but you've changed so much in the past year. I barely recognize you. You used to have passions! You were a man with convictions, you were lit from within…

VOINITSKY. Ha! I was lit from within, but nobody wanted any of my light.

(Pause.)

VOINITSKY. "Lit from within." That's a cruel thing to say. I'm forty-seven now. It's all over.

(pause)

Until this past year I was just like you—another pseudo-intellectual, eyes closed, trying not to see life for what it really is. I thought that was the right way to be. But God—now. If you only knew. I don't sleep at night, I'm so dissatisfied…I lie awake in bed fuming that I let all that time slip by! I'm an idiot. I could have had everything.

And now I'm old and I can't have anything.

SONYA. Uncle Vanya. This is boring.

MARIA VASILYEVNA. You blame your prior convictions. But they're not to blame. You yourself are to blame. You never understood that just having convictions doesn't lead to success. You should have *done* something!

VOINITSKY. Done something? We can't all be writing *perpetuum mobile* like your Herr Professor.

MARIA VASILYEVNA. So what's your point?

SONYA. *(pleading)* Grandmother. Uncle Vanya. Please.

VOINITSKY. I'll be quiet. I'll be quiet.

(Pause.)

VOINITSKY. Sorry.

(Pause.)

YELENA ANDREYEVNA. It's really nice out today.

Not too hot.

(Pause.)

VOINITSKY. Uh-huh.

Perfect weather for hanging yourself.

*(***TELEGIN*** tunes his guitar. **MARINA** walks around near the house and calls out to the chickens.)*

MARINA. Tseep tseep tseep…

SONYA. What did the peasants want, Nannechka?

MARINA. Same as always. It's that old piece of land again.

Tseep tseep tseep…

SONYA. Who are you looking for?

MARINA. Petrushka walked off with the chicks…I don't want the crows to find them…

(She exits.)

*(***TELEGIN*** plays a song on his guitar. Everyone listens in silence.)*

*(The song ends. **TELEGIN** lowers the guitar. A few seconds later, the **HIRED MAN** enters.)*

HIRED MAN. Is the doctor here?

*(to **ASTROV**)*

They've come for you, Mikhail Lvovich.

ASTROV. Jesus.

Where'd they come from?

HIRED MAN. The factory.

ASTROV. *(annoyed)* All right. Thank you.

(a short pause)

What can I do? I have to go.

(he looks for his hat)

Goddammit.

This is really annoying.

SONYA. I'm so sorry. Come back for dinner when you're done.

ASTROV. No, it'll be too late. What the...Where's my...

(to the **HIRED MAN***)*

You know what? Bring me a glass of vodka first.

(The **HIRED MAN** *exits.)*

ASTROV. Where is my godda—

(he finds his hat)

In one of his plays, Ostrovsky has a character with a big moustache and zero aptitude. That would be me.

Uh...

Goodbye, everyone.

(to **YELENA***)*

If you want to drop by at some point—with Sophia Alexandrovna of course—that would make me very happy. My estate isn't very big, but I have an orchard and a nice nursery...you won't find a better one for hundreds of versts, actually...oh, and there's a state forest nearby. The groundskeeper is old and sick so I pretty much manage the whole thing for him... anyway...

YELENA. Yes, I've been told that you love the forest. That's very sweet, but doesn't it interfere with your true calling? I mean, you're a doctor.

ASTROV. Only God knows about true callings.

YELENA. And you find it interesting?

ASTROV. Yes, the work is very interesting.

VOINITSKY. *(ironically)* Oh yes, very.

YELENA. But you're still so young...you look...what...thirty-six, thirty-seven...it can't possibly be as interesting as you say. A forest is just a lot of...trees. It seems pretty monotonous.

SONYA. Oh no! It's fascinating! Mikhail Lvovich plants a new forest every year, and they've already given him a bronze medal and a certificate for his work. He also petitions to save the older forests. If you talk to him about it, you'll end up completely agreeing with him. He says forests are the most beautiful things on earth and that they actually teach us what beauty *is*. They also inspire...um...they put us in a more spiritual mood. The forest tempers a harsh climate...and... in countries where the climate is gentle, people are kinder...they're more adaptable and attractive...their speech is elegant...they even move gracefully. Science and art flourish in these climates...their philosophy is enlightened, their attitude towards women is mature and evolved...

VOINITSKY. Bravo! That's all very nice, Sonya, but not particularly convincing.

(*to* **ASTROV**)

I will continue to burn firewood in my stove, thank you. And build wooden sheds if I need to.

ASTROV. You could use peat in your stove, and you could build your sheds out of stone. Listen, I can tolerate people chopping down a forest out of necessity, but why destroy all of them? The Russian forest is being decimated. Millions of trees perish, animals and birds have to look for a new place to live, rivers recede, this wonderful, sacred landscape is disappearing, and all on account of people like you who don't want to bend down and pick up their own fuel off the ground.

(*to* **YELENA**)

Don't you agree? You have to be a barbarian to take that kind of beauty and burn it up in your stove. Man has been blessed with reason and creativity, but instead of progressing, he only knows how to ruin. There are fewer and fewer forests, rivers are drying up, wildlife is being displaced, the climate is changing, and every day the land becomes less fertile and more disgraceful.

(to VOINITSKY*)*

You're giving me an ironic look. You're not taking anything I say seriously. And...and you know what, maybe I'm crazy. But when I walk through a forest that I saved, when I hear the sound of wind rustling in young trees, trees that I planted myself, I realize that I have my own little bit of control over the climate. And if after thousands of years one person is happier because of it, well then...

(he sighs)

I can't tell you the feeling I get when I plant a birch tree and I see it grow up and sprout leaves, I...I mean, I fill up with pride, I...

(seeing the HIRED MAN, *who has brought him a glass of vodka on a tray)*

But then again...

(drinking)

It's time for me to go.

Maybe I'm just crazy.

Goodbye.

(He heads towards the house. SONYA *takes him by the arm and walks with him.)*

SONYA. When will you come to see us again?

ASTROV. I'm not sure.

SONYA. Are we going to have to wait another month?

(They walk into the house. MARIA VASILYEVNA *and* TELEGIN *remain by the table;* YELENA ANDREYEVNA *and* VOINITSKY *go off to the verandah.)*

YELENA. Ivan Petrovich. You behaved like a child. Did you have to insult my husband in front of Maria Vasilyevna? And today you picked a fight with him at breakfast. It's so petty.

VOINITSKY. Well. I hate him.

YELENA. It's pointless to hate Alexander. He's the same as all of us. He's no worse than you.

VOINITSKY. Akh, if only you could see your face right now. And the way you move. The laziness! You could care less...

YELENA. Fine, fine, I'm lazy and I'm boring.

You know, everyone makes fun of Alexander and pretends to pity me. Poor thing, she has an old husband! But I see past it. It's just like Astrov said. Man will indiscriminately destroy the forest until there's nothing left. It's the same thing when you pick people apart and try to make sure that there there's no purity or self-sacrifice left in them. Why can't you make peace with a woman who isn't yours? The doctor is right—the demon of destruction is inside all of you. You don't care about the forest, you don't care about the birds, and you don't actually care about me.

VOINITSKY. I don't like it when you philosophize.

(Pause.)

YELENA. The doctor has a tired, anxious face. An interesting face.

Sonya likes him. Obviously. She's in love with him.

Since I've been here he's come to visit three different times, but, you know, I get shy around him. We've never had a real conversation.

Maybe I haven't been nice enough.

Maybe he thinks I'm mean.

That's why we're friends, Ivan Petrovich. We're both tedious, boring people.

Don't look at me like that.

VOINITSKY. How do you want me to look at you? I'm in love with you. You're my only happiness. You're my youth. I know there's almost no chance you'll ever love me back, zero chance even, but I don't need anything from you. I just want to look at you and listen to your voice…

YELENA. Shh. Someone could hear you!

(They go to the house.)

VOINITSKY. *(walking behind her)* Just let me talk to you about my love. Don't run away. That would be the closest thing to happiness for me.

YELENA. This is excruciating.

(They both go into the house. TELEGIN plays the guitar. MARIA VASILYEVNA makes a note in the margins of her pamphlet.)

(Curtain.)

ACT TWO

(A dining room in **SEREBRYAKOV**'s *house. Night. A watchman can be heard tapping his stick outside.)*

*(***SEREBRYAKOV*** *sits in an armchair in front of an open window and dozes.* **YELENA ANDREYEVNA** *sits by his side and also dozes.)*

SEREBRYAKOV. *(waking up)* Who's there?

Sonya, is that you?

YELENA. …It's me.

SEREBRYAKOV. Lenochka.

The pain is unbearable.

YELENA. Your blanket fell on the floor.

(She wraps the blanket around his legs.)

YELENA. I'll close the window.

SEREBRYAKOV. No, no, I can't breathe…

I dozed off and I dreamt that my left leg didn't belong to me.

The pain woke me up. Excruciating pain. This can't be gout. It has to be rheumatism.

What time is it?

YELENA. Past midnight.

(Pause.)

SEREBRYAKOV. Tomorrow morning go look in the library for Batyushkov. I think I saw him there.

YELENA. Huh?

SEREBRYAKOV. Look for Batyushkov in the morning. Remember? We had a copy.

Why am I having such a hard time breathing?

YELENA. You're tired. You haven't slept for two nights.

SEREBRYAKOV. They say Turgenev developed angina from gout.

(pause)

Old age is so goddamn repulsive. When I got old, I started repulsing myself. And everyone else too. You all must find it repulsive to even look at me.

YELENA. You make it seem like it's our fault that you're old.

SEREBRYAKOV. And you. You, more than anyone...you find me repulsive.

(YELENA walks some distance away and takes a seat.)

SEREBRYAKOV. Oh, come on. I'm not stupid. I understand. You're young, healthy, beautiful...you want to live, and I'm an old man, nearly a corpse. You think I don't know? I should be dead by now. It's embarrassing that I'm still alive. But just wait. You'll be free of me soon enough.

YELENA. I'm so tired...

Can we be quiet for a little while?

SEREBRYAKOV. And of course thanks to me everyone is exhausted and bored and unfulfilled. You're all wasting your youth and I'm perfectly content and delighted to be alive. Yes. Fine. Of course!

YELENA. Be quiet! You're torturing me!

SEREBRYAKOV. Of course. I torture everyone.

YELENA. *(through tears)* This is horrible. What do you want from me?

(After a short pause:)

SEREBRYAKOV. Nothing.

YELENA. Well then stop talking.

SEREBRYAKOV. It's the strangest thing. If Ivan Petrovich is talking or even that old bitch, Maria Vasilyevna, it's nothing, it's fine, people listen, rapt, but if I start talking, if I say a single word, everyone looks utterly *despondent*. Even my voice is repulsive. Well fine. Let's say I am disgusting. Let's say I am an egotistical bastard. Don't I have the right to be egotistical in my old age? Haven't I earned that much for myself? I'm asking you, Yelena! Do I not have the right to a peaceful old age and a little attention?

YELENA. No one is disputing your rights.

(The window slams in the wind.)

YELENA. I'm closing the window.

(She closes it.)

YELENA. It's going to rain.

No one is disputing your rights.

(A pause. The watchman taps his stick in the yard and sings a song. They listen to it.)

SEREBRYAKOV. You don't know what it's like. To spend your whole life at the university, to have an office and a lecture hall and colleagues...and then to suddenly out of nowhere find yourself living in this *crypt*, forced to listen to a bunch of idiots sitting around having pointless conversations...

I still want to live—I still want fame and success and to—to feel like I'm part of something important! This is like living in exile. I spend every minute longing for the past, obsessing over other people's success, fearing death... I can't do it much longer. I don't have the strength. And on top of it everyone hates me for being old!

YELENA. Hang in there. In five or six years I'll be old too.

(SONYA enters.)

SONYA. Papa, you told us to send for Doctor Astrov, but now that he's here, you refuse to see him. It's inconsiderate. He's gone to all this trouble.

SEREBRYAKOV. What do I need Astrov for? He knows as much about medicine as I do about astronomy.

SONYA. So what do you want? The entire medical faculty to come write a prescription for your gout?

SEREBRYAKOV. That man is a joke. I have nothing to say to him.

SONYA. Fine. Whatever you want.

(she sits down)

I don't care anymore.

SEREBRYAKOV. What time is it now?

YELENA. Almost one.

SEREBRYAKOV. It's so stuffy in here.

Sonya, bring me my drops.

The ones on the table.

SONYA. Hold on...

(She looks for a while, then finds them and hands them to him.)

SEREBRYAKOV. *(irritated)* Akh, no, not those! Goddammit! I can't ask for anything!

SONYA. Don't be rude. Maybe some people respond to it, but not me. I don't like it. I don't have time for it. I have to get up early tomorrow and cut hay.

(VOINITSKY enters in a robe, holding a candle.)

VOINITSKY. There's a storm coming.

(The crack of thunder and then lightning.)

VOINITSKY. There it is.

Hélène, Sonya, go to bed. I've come to relieve you.

SEREBRYAKOV. *(frightened)* No! Don't leave me here with him! He'll talk to me!

VOINITSKY. They need sleep. This is the second night in a row you've kept them up.

SEREBRYAKOV. Fine, fine, they can go, but you have to leave too. Thank you for offering, but I beg you, in the name of our former friendship, please go away. We'll talk later.

VOINITSKY. *(grinning)* Our *former* friendship.

SONYA. Be quiet, Uncle Vanya.

SEREBRYAKOV. *(to his wife)* My darling, don't leave me here with him! He'll talk my ear off.

VOINITSKY. This is hilarious.

(MARINA enters with a candle.)

SONYA. Oh, Nannechka. You need to go to bed.

MARINA. But the samovar is still on the table.

SEREBRYAKOV. Yes, no one sleeps, everyone is exhausted, and I'm having the time of my life!!

MARINA. *(walking up to SEREBRYAKOV, gently)* What is it, sweetie? Are you in pain? My legs ache too. Ooh. You wouldn't believe how they ache.

(adjusting the blanket)

You've been sick for a long time now. Vera Petrovna, may she rest in peace, Sonyechka's mother, she used to lose sleep at night, worrying about you...she loved you so much...

(Pause.)

MARINA. Old people are like children, all they want is a little pity. Isn't that right? But they don't give us enough of it. Never enough.

(She kisses SEREBRYAKOV on the shoulder.)

Let's go to bed, sweetie pie. I'll tuck you in. Come on. Let's go, you shining star. I'll make you some linden tea and then we'll warm up your little legs. And after you fall asleep I'll say a prayer.

SEREBRYAKOV. *(touched)* All right. Let's go.

MARINA. My legs ache too. Oooh. It's a terrible feeling, isn't it?

(leads him away together with SONYA)

Vera Petrovna loved you so much. She was always worried about you. You were just a tiny baby back then,

Sonyechka. A silly little thing. Come on, that's right, come this way...you're such a special special man...

(SEREBRYAKOV, SONYA and MARINA exit.)

YELENA. He completely exhausts me. I can barely stand up.

VOINITSKY. Yeah, well, I exhaust myself. This is the third night in a row I haven't slept.

YELENA. There's something wrong with this house. Your mother hates everything except for the Professor and her pamphlets; the Professor is a mess—he doesn't trust me and he's scared of you; Sonya is angry with her father and angry with me—she hasn't spoken to me in two weeks—and you hate my husband and treat your mother like garbage.

I'm going insane. I almost burst into tears twenty times today. There's something seriously wrong with this house.

VOINITSKY. You're philosophizing again.

YELENA. You're an educated man, Ivan Petrovich. You of all people should understand that the world isn't a terrible place because of robberies and—and—and fires—it's all the hatred and rivalry and petty squabbles. You need to stop complaining and start trying harder to make peace in your family.

VOINITSKY. First I'd have to make peace with myself.

(throwing himself at her hand)

My darling...

YELENA. Oh, stop it.

(taking her hand away)

Get away from me!

VOINITSKY. Soon it'll stop raining, and everything outside will be clean and refreshed. But not me. There's this thought that I can't get out of my head. It haunts me. It's always quietly suffocating me.

The thought that my life has been...irretrievably...lost.

The past is gone, it was wasted on trivialities, and the present...God, the present is too ridiculous for words.

Look: here is my life. Here is my love for you. Where do you want me to put it? What do you want me to do with it? These are my deepest, truest feelings, and they're perishing, like a ray of sunshine that's fallen on a ditch.

YELENA. When you talk about your love for me, I just...I go completely blank. I'm sorry. I have nothing to say.

(starting to leave)

Good night.

VOINITSKY. *(blocking her way)* The part that kills me, the part that really kills me, is the fact that another life is being wasted in this house, in the room right next to mine. What are you waiting for? What kind of crazy philosophical argument can you make in your defense? You have to understand—

YELENA. *(looking at him intently)* You're drunk, Ivan Petrovich.

VOINITSKY. It's possible.

It's possible.

YELENA. Where's the doctor?

VOINITSKY. He's here. He's spending the night with me.

It's possible, it's possible...anything is possible...

YELENA. So you drank too much again. Why are you doing this?

VOINITSKY. When I'm drunk life seems more like life.

Don't try and stop me, Hélène!

YELENA. You never used to drink this much. Akh, you never used to talk this much either.

Go to bed. You're boring me.

VOINITSKY. *(throwing himself at her hand again)* My darling... my strange little wonder!

YELENA. Please. Leave me alone.

This. *This* is repulsive.

(She leaves.)

VOINITSKY. *(alone)* ...And she's gone.

(Pause.)

VOINITSKY. I met her ten years ago, at my sister's house. She was seventeen, and I was thirty-seven. Why didn't I fall in love with her then and propose to her that night? It would have been possible. She'd be my wife now. Yes. Right now the storm would be waking us up, and she'd be frightened, and I'd hold her in my arms and whisper: "Don't be scared. I'm right here." Just thinking about it makes me so happy, see, I'm laughing...but then I get so confused...why am I old? Why doesn't she love me back? Akh, and her lame rhetoric...her lazy morality...her pretentious thoughts about the end of the world...I find all of those things despicable.

(Pause.)

VOINITSKY. I was lied to. I loved the Professor, I loved that pathetic, gout-ridden man, I worked like an ox for him. Sonya and I squeezed every last drop out of this estate; we lived like peasants; we sold vegetable oil and beans and cheese and nearly starved to death so we could save every kopeck and send it to him. Oh, and I was so proud of him. I lived and breathed for him. Everything he wrote, everything he said was a work of genius to me. God. And now? He's retired and I can step back and look at the sum total of his life: he won't be survived by a single sheet of paper. He's completely unknown, he's nothing. A soap bubble. So I was lied to.

I see that now.

I was a fool.

(ASTROV enters in his frock coat, without his waistcoat or his tie. He's tipsy. TELEGIN *follows him with the guitar.)*

ASTROV. Play!

TELEGIN. Uh. Sir. Everyone is sleeping.

ASTROV. Play!

*(*TELEGIN *begins to play, quietly.)*

ASTROV. *(to* VOINITSKY*)* You alone? No ladies?

(arms akimbo, he quietly sings)

'ходи хата

ходи печь

хозяину негде лечь...'

The thunder woke me up.

This is some downpour.

What time is it?

VOINITSKY. Who the hell cares.

ASTROV. I thought I heard Yelena Andreyevna.

VOINITSKY. She was just here.

ASTROV. She's a gorgeous woman.

(He looks at all the vials on the table.)

ASTROV. Medicine. He's got every prescription in the world. Here's one from Kharkov...Moscow...Tula...

Is he sick or pretending?

VOINITSKY. He's sick.

(Pause.)

ASTROV. Why do you look so depressed? You feel bad for him?

VOINITSKY. Leave me alone.

ASTROV. Or could it be that you're in love with his wife?

VOINITSKY. She's my friend.

ASTROV. Already, huh?

VOINITSKY. What do you mean—already?

ASTROV. Women and men can only become friends in this
order: first acquaintances, then lovers, then friends.

VOINITSKY. That's a pretty vulgar thing to say.

ASTROV. How so? All right, fine, I'm feeling kind of vulgar.
You see, I'm drunk. I get drunk like this about once
a month. And when I'm this drunk, I'm shameless.
Nothing is sacred. I take on the most difficult
operations and I perform them brilliantly...I come
up with vague and impossibly beautiful plans for the
future...when I'm this drunk I stop feeling like a
creep and I start believing that I provide an enormous
service to mankind. Enormous! At times like this I
have my own perfect philosophical order and all of
you, my brothers, appear to be tiny insects...microbes.

   (*to* **TELEGIN**)

   Play, Waffles! Play!

TELEGIN. My dear friend, uh, you know I'd be happy to,
but you have to understand...people are sleeping!

ASTROV. Play!

   (**TELEGIN** *quietly begins to play again.*)

ASTROV. Let's have a drink. I think there's some cognac
left. And then when the sun comes up we'll go to my
place. *Shahll* we? I have this paramedic who always says
"shahll we" instead of "shall we." He's an asshole.

   Shahll we?

   (**SONYA** *enters. He sees her.*)

ASTROV. Excuse me. I forgot my necktie.

   (**ASTROV** *exits quickly.* **TELEGIN** *follows behind him.*)

SONYA. Uncle Vanya. You got drunk with the doctor again.
He's always been like that, but at your age—

   It doesn't suit you.

VOINITSKY. Age doesn't matter. When you have no life, you
live in your imagination. It's better than nothing.

SONYA. Well, that's wonderful. The hay has been cut, it's raining, everything is rotting, and you're living in your imagination. You've abandoned your work. And now I have to do everything by myself. I'm running out of energy, you know.

(*startled*)

Uncle, you have tears in your eyes!

VOINITSKY. Tears? No, it's nothing...it's silly...

The way you looked at me just now...you were exactly like your mother.

(*he kisses her face and hands hungrily*)

My sister...my sweet sister...where is she now? If she only knew. Akh, if she only knew!

SONYA. Knew what?

VOINITSKY. That it's so—the misery, the—

Nothing.

After all the...

Nothing.

I'll go now.

(*He leaves.*)

(**SONYA** *knocks on the door.*)

SONYA. Mikhail Lvovich! Are you still awake? I need to talk to you for a minute!

ASTROV. (*from behind the door*) Hold on!

(*He enters in his waistcoat and necktie.*)

What, uh...what can I do for you?

SONYA. Listen, you can drink all you want if that makes you happy, but please. Don't get my uncle drunk. It's not good for him.

ASTROV. Fine.

We won't drink anymore.

(*Pause.*)

ASTROV. Uh…I'm going home. It's already decided. By the time the horses are ready, it'll already be light outside.

SONYA. But it's still raining.

ASTROV. Nah, it's almost over, I'll just catch the end of it. It's time for me to go. And uh…maybe don't invite me to come see your father anymore. I keep telling him it's gout, he keeps saying it's rheumatism…I ask him to lie down, he sits up…then today he refused to talk to me at all.

SONYA. He's spoiled.

(looking through the sideboard)

Are you hungry? I might have a little snack.

ASTROV. Feel free.

SONYA. I love a late-night snack. Ooh, look, there are leftovers. You know, they say that my father had too much success with women and that's what spoiled him. Here, have some cheese.

(They both stand at the sideboard and eat together.)

ASTROV. This is the first thing I've eaten all day.

Your father is kind of a, uh…he's a difficult guy.

(he takes a bottle from the buffet)

May I?

(he pours himself a glass and drinks it)

All right, since it's just us, I'm going to speak candidly. I wouldn't survive a month in this house. I'd suffocate. You've got your father…he only cares about his gout and his books…you've got Uncle Vanya and his depression…your grandmother…and that stepmother of yours…

SONYA. What about my stepmother?

ASTROV. Everything about a person should be beautiful— her face and clothes, but also her soul and her thoughts. Your stepmother is good-looking, I won't argue with that…but all she does is eat, sleep, take walks, and enchant people with her beauty. Her life has no purpose. She has no responsibilities, other people do the work for her...that's how it is, right? And I think a life of leisure is a life wasted.

(Pause.)

ASTROV. Maybe I'm being too harsh. I'm dissatisfied, just like your Uncle Vanya, and we're both turning into old curmudgeons.

SONYA. You're really that dissatisfied with your life?

ASTROV. Listen, in general, I love life. But life in this part of the world, I mean this particular Russian, philistine, country existence...I can't stand it anymore. I hate it. And if we're talking about my personal life...I mean, God, there's nothing to be said about it. Nothing good, anyway. You know when you're walking in the woods on a dark night...and you see a light shining far off in the distance...and you think to yourself: even though I'm tired and it's dark and the branches are scratching my face...everything is gonna be okay... because I have that light? And I'll get there eventually?

Well, I work—you know this—I work harder than anyone else in this county. I mean, I'm beaten down, Sonya, I suffer unbearably...but I have no light in the distance. I can't see anything up ahead. I no longer expect anything of myself, and I don't think I'm capable of really loving people.

It's been such a long time since I've felt real love for anyone.

SONYA. You don't love *anyone?*

ASTROV. No one. I mean, I feel a certain fondness for your Nanny, but that's a kind of nostalgia. See, the peasants I meet are all totally backward and they live in filth, but I find it even harder to get along with educated people. It's so tiring. Everyone we know— all of our supposed *friends*—they're consumed by petty thoughts and petty feelings and they can't see past their own noses. The truth is, educated people are often pretty stupid. And then the smart ones can be the most insufferable...they get hysterical, they analyze themselves to death...they whine and gossip and say terrible things about each other and then when they meet someone new they scrutinize him and say, you know, "oh, he's a psychopath," or, you know, "he's so pretentious." And when they can't find a label to stick to my forehead they say something like: "He's strange. There's just something a little strange about him."

I love the forest, I guess that's strange. I don't eat meat...I guess that makes me strange.

We've lost any kind of pure, immediate connection with nature. Or with each other. No thank you. Not for me.

(He wants a drink. **SONYA** *tries to stop him.)*

ASTROV. What's that about?

SONYA. It just...it doesn't suit you. You're so refined, you have such a gentle voice...you're...you're not like anyone else I know...you're wonderful. Who wants to be like those people who get drunk and play cards all day? Please, stop drinking. You always say that instead of creating, mankind destroys. So then why would you destroy yourself and your beautiful—there's no reason to do it. Please, please, I'm begging you, stop drinking.

ASTROV. *(extending his hand to her)* Done. I won't drink anymore.

SONYA. Give me your word.

ASTROV. You have my word.

SONYA. *(squeezing his hand tightly)* Thank you!

ASTROV. Basta! I've sobered up. See? I'm already sober and I will remain so for the rest of my days.

(he looks at the clock)

All right. To sum up: my time has passed. It's too late for me...I'm older now, I'm overworked, I've gotten a little coarse, I feel numb all the time, and I don't get attached to people. I don't love anybody and...that's it. I won't love anybody until I die.

What still gets me is beauty. I'm not indifferent to beauty. If Yelena Andreyevna wanted to, she could make my head spin...but see, that, that's not love, that's not real attachment, that's...

(He covers his eyes with his hands and shudders.)

SONYA. What's wrong?

ASTROV. It's uh...

I had a patient die under chloroform. During Lent.

SONYA. You need to forget about that.

(Pause.)

SONYA. Mikhail Lvovich. I'm...I'm just curious about something. If I had a friend, or a, or a...younger sister, and you found out she...well, let's just say...let's say that she...that she loved you. How would you react?

ASTROV. I don't know. I guess I would try to help her understand that I couldn't love her back...and I'd tell her I'm not interested in that kind of thing anymore.

(a short pause)

Aaanyway. If I'm really going I need to go now. Let's say goodbye, sweetheart, or next thing we know it'll be morning.

(squeezing her hand)

I'll go through the living room...otherwise your uncle might find me and try to keep me here.

(He exits.)

SONYA. *(alone)* He didn't tell me anything, not really...

His heart is closed off. So then why do I feel so happy?

(she laughs with joy)

I told him that he was refined, with a gentle voice...did I really say that? Oh god. It's true, his voice has this way of quivering in the…it's like he's touching me when he talks…I can still feel him in the air…

(wringing her hands)

It's horrible. Why am I not pretty? And I know it…I know I'm not pretty.

Last Sunday when we were leaving church, I heard a woman say: "She's kind and she has a good personality, but she's just not pretty…it's a shame." Not pretty…

(Enter YELENA ANDREYEVNA.*)*

YELENA. *(opening the window)* The rain stopped.

The air feels amazing.

(Pause.)

YELENA. Where's the doctor?

SONYA. He's gone.

(Pause.)

YELENA. Sophie!

SONYA. What.

YELENA. When are you going to stop being mad at me? Neither of us did anything wrong. Why do we have to be enemies? It's too much…

SONYA. …I wanted to make up, but I…

(she embraces YELENA*)*

No more being angry.

YELENA. Well—good!

(They are both moved and excited.)

SONYA. Did Papa go to bed?

YELENA. No. He's sitting in the living room.

Sometimes we go weeks without speaking to each other. God knows why.

(seeing that the sideboard is open)

What's this?

SONYA. Mikhail Lvovich wanted a snack.

YELENA. There's wine...come on. Let's drink *Bruderschaft*.

SONYA. Yes!

YELENA. From one glass...

> *(she pours it)*
>
> It's better this way.
>
> So, I can call you "Ты"?

SONYA. Ты.

> *(They interlock their arms, drink, and kiss.)*

SONYA. I've wanted to make up for a long time, but I was ashamed, I guess...

> *(She starts crying.)*

YELENA. Why are you crying?

SONYA. I don't know. I'm just crying.

YELENA. That happens...

> *(She starts crying.)*
>
> You nut. Now you're making me cry.
>
> *(They cry together. After a pause:)*

YELENA. You're mad at me because you think I married your father for the wrong reasons. I swear on my life: I married him for love. I was captivated by him. He was this famous scholar, and I...I mean, it wasn't real love, I know that now, but at the time it seemed totally real to me. There was nothing I could do. And ever since the wedding you've been giving me these horrible *looks*. You have such intelligent, suspicious eyes.

SONYA. Let's make up and forget all about it.

YELENA. You can't approach the world that way—it doesn't look good on you. You have to trust people. I know it's hard, but otherwise life is unbearable.

> *(Pause.)*

SONYA. Tell me something, as a friend.

> And be honest.

Are you happy?

YELENA. No.

SONYA. I knew it! All right. One more question. Answer honestly. Would you...I mean if you could, would you want a younger husband?

YELENA. You're such a little girl. Of course I would!

(laughing)

Ask me something else.

SONYA. Do you like the doctor?

YELENA. Very much.

SONYA. *(laughing)* I must look so stupid right now...it's obvious, isn't it? He's gone, but I can still hear his footsteps and his voice...

I look in the dark windows and I think I see his face there, looking back at me. Oh god. I need to talk to someone about this. But we have to be quiet...it's so humiliating. Let's go to my room. Am I acting like an idiot? Be honest. Tell me something about him...

YELENA. What do you want me to say?

SONYA. He's smart...he know about everything, he can do anything...he heals people, he plants forests...

YELENA. He's smart...but it's more than just medicine and forests. Sweetie, he's a genius. He's brave...he's free-thinking...he has a *vision*...

To plant a sapling and then to actually care about what happens to it a thousand years from now...to think that hard about the future of humanity... People like him are rare, and they deserve love...of course he drinks, and he's a little vulgar...but what's so bad about that? He's Russian. He's talented. He's not going to be a Puritan. Think about what his life is like! He travels on muddy roads, across great distances, through blizzards and rain...working with people who are dirty and sick and needy...I think it would be impossible to stay clean and sober for very long.

(she kisses **SONYA***)*

You deserve happiness.

I wish you happiness, from the bottom of my heart.

(she stands)

Me, I'm boring. I'm...I'm like a minor character in a play. With my music, in this house, in all my love affairs...for my whole life, I've always been a minor character.

Just between the two of us, Sonya—when I think about it, I am very, very unhappy!

(She walks around the stage, agitated.)

Nothing makes me happy.

No! Why are you laughing?

SONYA. *(laughing, covering her face)* I don't know. I can't help it. I'm so happy!

YELENA. I want to play something.

I want to play something right now.

SONYA. Play.

(embracing her)

I can't sleep anyway. Play!

YELENA. Wait. Your father is still up. When he feels sick, music irritates him. Go ask him if it's all right, and then I'll play.

SONYA. I'll be right back.

(She exits.)

(The watchman taps outside.)

YELENA. I haven't played in ages.

I'll play and I'll cry. I'll cry like a fool.

(out the window)

Are you making that noise, Yefim?

VOICE OF THE WATCHMAN. Yep! It's me!

YELENA. You have to stop. The Professor's not feeling well.

VOICE OF THE WATCHMAN. All right. I'll go.

(whistling)

Come on, doggies! Zjuchka, Malchik! Zjuchka!

(A long pause.)

(SONYA *returns.)*

SONYA. ...He said no.

(Curtain.)

ACT THREE

(The living room in **SEREBRYAKOV**'s *house. Three doors: one on the right, one on the left, and one center.)*

(Mid-day.)

*(***VOINITSKY** *and* **SONYA** *are sitting.* **YELENA** *walks around the room, lost in thought.)*

VOINITSKY. Herr Professor has graciously requested that we all meet in this room at one o'clock.

(looking at his watch)

It's quarter till.

He wants to Make An Announcement.

YELENA. Maybe it's about a new project.

VOINITSKY. Oh come on. He doesn't have any projects. He writes gibberish and he bitches and complains. That's it.

SONYA. *(rebuking him)* Uncle!

VOINITSKY. Sorry, sorry.

(pointing to **YELENA**)

Ha. Look at this one. She's just *reeling* from boredom.

Cute, my dear. Very cute!

YELENA. Well you buzz around this house all day like a fly. Don't you ever get tired?

(with great melancholy)

And I am bored. I'm dying of boredom. I don't know what to do.

SONYA. *(shrugging)* There's plenty to do around here. If you're up for it.

YELENA. For instance...?

SONYA. You could help out around the house. You could teach. You could nurse the sick and the dying. Before you and Papa came, Uncle Vanya and I would go to the market and sell flour.

YELENA. Well. Fine. But I don't know how to do any of that.

Anyway, it's not interesting. That kind of thing only happens in ideological novels.

(a short pause)

I mean, someone like me, someone who's...what, I should go knock on people's doors and offer to miraculously heal and teach them?

SONYA. You could teach! I don't understand why you won't even try it. You'd get used to it after a while.

(embraces her)

Don't be bored.

(laughing)

I know, you don't know what to do with yourself, but boredom is contagious. Look: Uncle Vanya doesn't do anything anymore...he follows you around like a shadow. I abandon my chores just to talk to you—I can't help it. We used to have to beg the doctor to come see us, and now he's here almost every day. He's forgotten all about his patients and his forest. You've put us all under your spell. You're like a witch!

VOINITSKY. See? There's no reason to lie around feeling bad for yourself.

(getting excited)

Come on, you clever girl...think about it! You have mermaid blood flowing through your veins, so be a mermaid! Let yourself go for once in your life...find yourself a merman and plop head over heels into the ocean! Leave Herr Professor and the rest of us standing on the shore, arms outstretched...

YELENA. *(furious)* Leave me alone! This is cruel...

*(She tries to leave. **VOINITSKY** doesn't let her.)*

VOINITSKY. No, no, no, I'm sorry, my only joy, forgive me...I'm sorry.

(he kisses her hand)

I'm sorry.

YELENA. An angel wouldn't have the patience for this.

VOINITSKY. I'll bring you some roses as a peace offering. I gathered a bouquet for you this morning. Autumn roses—lovely, sad roses...

(He exits.)

YELENA. Autumn roses—lovely, sad roses.

(YELENA and SONYA look out the window.)

YELENA. It's September already.

How are we going to get through the winter?

(Pause.)

YELENA. Where's the doctor?

SONYA. In Uncle Vanya's room. He's writing something. Listen, I'm glad Uncle Vanya left...I need to talk to you.

YELENA. What about?

SONYA. God. What about.

(She lays her head on YELENA's chest.)

YELENA. Ohhh. Now, now...

(she strokes SONYA's hair)

Enough, enough...

SONYA. I'm not pretty.

YELENA. You have beautiful hair.

SONYA. No!

(looking around, then finding a mirror)

No.

When a woman isn't pretty, people always say: "You have beautiful eyes." Or "you have beautiful hair." I've loved him for six years now.

I love him more than my own mother.

I hear him everywhere...I feel his hand pressing into mine...I sit and I stare at the door, convinced he's about to walk in...

That's it...and I keep running to you to talk about it. He comes to visit every day, but he barely looks at me...he doesn't see me...and I...I'm in agony. I'm losing hope.

(in despair)

I used to be strong, and now I...I stay up all night praying...I walk up to him and make these pathetic attempts to start a conversation...I look him right in the eyes and I...I have no pride left, I can't control myself...yesterday I told Uncle Vanya...all the servants know. Everyone knows.

YELENA. Does he know?

SONYA. No.

He doesn't notice me.

YELENA. *(thinking)* He's a strange man.

You know what? Let me talk to him.

I'll be very careful, I'll just drop a few hints...

(Pause.)

YELENA. Really, how long can you stay like this? Not knowing?

Let me talk to him.

*(**SONYA** nods.)*

YELENA. He either loves you or he doesn't—it won't be hard to find out. Oh sweetie, don't look so worried...I'll be so careful, he won't even know what's happening.

All we need to find out is: yes or no?

(Pause.)

YELENA. If the answer is no, he shouldn't come here anymore. Agreed?

(SONYA nods.)

YELENA. It would be easier if you didn't see him all the time. We'll find out right now. He wanted to show me some of his drawings anyway. Go get him. Tell him I want to talk to him.

SONYA. *(getting excited, worked up)* You'll tell me the truth? You won't lie to me?

YELENA. Of course. I think the truth, whatever it turns out to be, is never as frightening as uncertainty. Trust me, sweetie.

SONYA. All right.

All right!

I'll…I'll tell him you want to see him…

(She goes to the door and then pauses.)

SONYA. Maybe not knowing is better. Then at least you have hope.

YELENA. What?

SONYA. Nothing.

(She exits.)

YELENA. *(alone)* There's nothing worse than knowing someone's secret and not being able to help.

(thinking)

He's not in love with her, that's obvious, but he should marry her anyway. She's not beautiful, but for someone his age…a country doctor…she would be a perfect wife. She's smart, she's kind, she's got a good heart… no, that's not it…it's…

(Pause.)

YELENA. I understand her. Poor thing. Living in a place like this…everything is so desperately boring…instead of people there are these grey spots wandering around, having banal conversations…the only thing that matters is what they had to eat or drink or how long they slept…and then he comes along…so different…

interesting, handsome, a good talker...like a bright moon in a dark sky...it would be so easy to succumb to someone like him, to forget everything...I guess I'm a little captivated myself.

Yes. I feel bored when he's not around...I'm smiling now, just thinking about him...

And Uncle Vanya says I have mermaid blood.

"Let yourself go for once in your life..."

Is that what I should do? Open the cage, fly away from all of you...from your tired faces, from the boring conversations...forget that any of you ever existed...

But I'm a coward. My conscience would torment me.

He comes here every day now, and I know why...I already feel guilty...I want to fall on my knees before Sonya and cry...

(ASTROV *enters with his maps.*)

ASTROV. Hello!

(*he takes her hand and presses it hello*)

You wanted to see my work?

YELENA. Yesterday you said you would show me—is now a bad time? Are you free?

ASTROV. Of course.

(*He unfurls the map on a card table and secures it with pushpins.*)

ASTROV. Where were you born?

YELENA. (*helping him*) Petersburg.

ASTROV. And where were you educated?

YELENA. At the conservatory.

ASTROV. Oh. Well. You probably won't find this very interesting.

YELENA. Why not? I don't know much about the countryside but I've read a lot...

ASTROV. Let's see. Well. I have a table here in the house...
in Ivan Petrovich's room. When I'm overtired, or fed
up with work, I drop everything and I hurry over here
and I spend hours amusing myself with this thing...

Ivan Petrovich and Sophia Alexandrovna work right
near me, clicking away at their accounts, and I sit at
my little table and I daub my little paintbrush and I
feel very warm and peaceful and I listen to the crickets
chirp outside...

But I don't allow myself this pleasure very often. About
once a month.

(he points to the map)

Now look. This is our district, the way it looked 50 years
ago. The dark green and the light green represent the
forest; you can see half of the entire district was forest.
The red cross-hatching on top of the green, that's where
the animals are...elk and goats and...I'm showing both
the flora and the fauna. This lake over here...this lake
had swans, geese, ducks...a whole heap of birds, the
old men used to say...just, you know, thousands and
thousands of birds...you can't even imagine...when
they were in flight it was like this giant black cloud...
okay...uh...In addition to the countryside and the
village you can see...scattered around are these little
settlements...tiny farms...homesteads, not estates...
here's a couple monasteries, there's a water mill...and
there were a lot of cattle and horses, everything was...
that's the blue. See, in this section, I applied the blue
very, uh...thickly...because there were entire herds,
and three horses in every yard.

(A pause.)

ASTROV. Now look down here.

This is a map of our district twenty-five years ago.

Now just a third of the district is covered by forest.
There are no goats anymore, there are just a few elk.

The green and the blue are faded. And so on and so on...

Now we come to the third part.

Our district at present.

The green is scattered now; it only exists in tiny patches. The elk are gone. The swans are gone. No more wood grouse. No more little homesteads or monasteries. This is a map of gradual and undeniable degradation, a degradation that will take about 10 to fifteen more years to complete. Now you might argue that this is progress, this is civilization, that the old has to step aside for the new...and I would understand that argument if in place of these forests there were paved roads or schools or train tracks...anything that made the population healthier or wealthier or smarter... but it's nothing of the kind. We still have the same swamps and mosquitoes and impassable roads, and there's more poverty and typhus and diptheria than ever...more fires...no, this degradation of the land is the result of man's pointless battle for survival; this degradation comes from ignorance, from a total lack of self-awareness, from freezing hungry sick people desperate to survive who instinctively and senselessly grab at anything that could relieve their hunger or provide warmth for their children...everything is destroyed in the name of survival and nobody thinks about the day after tomorrow. I mean, look. The land has been ruined. And nothing has been given back in return.

(coldly)

I can tell from your expression that you don't find this interesting at all.

YELENA. It's just...I understand very little about it, I—

ASTROV. There's nothing to understand. It's boring.

YELENA. Look, honestly, I'm distracted. Forgive me. I have to subject you to a kind of um...little interrogation, and I'm embarrassed, and I'm not sure how to begin.

ASTROV. An interrogation?

YELENA. Yes, an interrogation...but...an innocent one.

Let's sit!

(They sit.)

YELENA. It concerns a...a young lady. Let's see...I want us to talk honestly, as friends, and I'm not going to beat around the bush. So we'll have this conversation and then we won't speak of it again. All right?

ASTROV. Uh...sure.

YELENA. It's about my stepdaughter Sonya.

Do you like her?

ASTROV. Yes, I have a great deal of respect for her.

YELENA. Do you like her...as a woman?

ASTROV. *(not right away)* No.

YELENA. All right. Another two or three words...and this will be over. You haven't noticed anything?

ASTROV. Nothing.

YELENA. *(takes his hand)* I understand. You don't love her. I see it in your eyes.

But she's suffering. You have to understand that. And you have to stop coming here.

ASTROV. *(standing up)* That's fine. My time has passed. I'm too busy and I...

(shrugging uncomfortably)

I mean...when could I...

(He's totally confused and embarrassed.)

YELENA. Oof, what an unpleasant conversation. I've been so worried...well, this is a weight off my mind. Thank God it's over. We'll act like it never happened, but you...

You have to leave.

You're a smart man, you understand why...

(Pause.)

YELENA. Yes. Well, I'm blushing.

ASTROV. If you had told me this a month or two ago, I might've considered it. But now...

(he shrugs)

If she's suffering, then of course...

But there's one thing I still don't understand: why did *you* conduct this little interrogation?

(he looks her in the eyes and wags his finger)

You're very crafty.

YELENA. What does that mean?

ASTROV. Very, very crafty. All right, so maybe Sonya is suffering...I'll concede that point. But then why were *you* so eager to interrogate me?

(getting excited, interrupting her as she starts to speak)

Come on, don't look so surprised, you know perfectly well why I come here every day...you know who I'm coming to see...oh come on, you little vixen, don't look at me like that, I've been around the block before...

YELENA. *(bewildered)* Vixen? I don't understand what you're saying.

ASTROV. You're a wild little minx, aren't you...you require a live sacrifice! I haven't done anything for an entire month, I've dropped everything, that's how much I want you...oh, and stop pretending you don't love this kind of attention...this is very appealing to you, this is just want you wanted...and what happens next? You've defeated me. You already knew that before you conducted your little interrogation.

(He bends over, head down, arms crossed.)

ASTROV. I submit. Take me, bite into my head!

YELENA. You're out of our mind.

ASTROV. *(laughing through his teeth)* Oh ho. You're being coy.

YELENA. I'm better than you think. I will not stoop to...I swear to you...

*(She tries to leave. **ASTROV** blocks her way.)*

ASTROV. Listen, I'll leave today, I won't come back again...
but...

(taking her hand, glancing around)

Where can we meet? Tell me quickly: where? Someone
could walk in...

(passionately)

God, you're wonderful...you're so *luxurious*...it's...

One kiss.

Let me kiss your hair, I want to smell it, I want to—

YELENA. I swear to you, I...

ASTROV. *(stopping her from speaking)* Why swear? There's no
need to swear. We don't have to talk about it. You're so
beautiful. Look at your hands!

(He kisses her hands.)

YELENA. That's enough. That's...leave.

(taking her hands away)

You've...you've forgotten yourself.

ASTROV. Just say it. Say it! Where will we meet tomorrow?

(he takes her by the waist)

It's inevitable. We have to see each other.

(He kisses her, and at the same time **VOINITSKY** *enters
with a bouquet of roses. He comes to a stop at the door.)*

YELENA. *(not seeing* **VOINITSKY***)* Oh god, spare me, please...
leave me alone...

(She gives in for a second and presses her head against
ASTROV*'s chest, breathing him in, and then:)*

YELENA. No!

(She tries to leave.)

ASTROV. *(holding her by the waist)* Come to the forest
tomorrow...two o'clock. Yes?

Yes?

Will you come?

(YELENA finally sees VOINITSKY.)

YELENA. Let go of me!

(She walks towards the window, humiliated.)

YELENA. This is horrible.

(VOINITSKY places the bouquet on a chair, then wipes his face and collar with a handkerchief.)

VOINITSKY. It's nothing…of course…it's nothing.

ASTROV. *(gloomy)* Hello, Ivan Petrovich. Weather's not bad today. It was cloudy in the morning, looked like it might rain for a while, but now the sun is out. It's been a nice autumn…and the crops are doing well this year…

(he rolls up the map into a tube)

I guess the only downside is the days are shorter.

(He exits.)

YELENA. *(quickly approaching VOINITSKY)* You have to help me…my husband and I need to leave this house. We need to leave today. Are you listening to me? Today!

VOINITSKY. *(wiping his face)* What? Fine. Good. Whatever you want.

I saw everything, Hélène. Everything.

YELENA. *(agitated)* Are you listening to me? We need to leave today!

(Enter SEREBRYAKOV, SONYA, TELEGIN and MARINA.)

TELEGIN. Well, to be honest, Your Excellency, I'm not in perfect health. I've been sick for two days now. My head is little—

SEREBRYAKOV. Where is everyone?

This house. It's like a labyrinth. Twenty-six rooms, you can never find anyone.

(ringing the bell)

Tell Maria Vasilyevna and Yelena Andreyevna to come immediately!

YELENA. I'm right here.

SEREBRYAKOV. Please, everyone, sit.

(SONYA walks up to YELENA.)

SONYA. What did he say?

YELENA. Let's talk about it later.

SONYA. You're shaking!

You're upset?

(looking searchingly at YELENA's face)

I understand.

He said he won't come here anymore.

Yes?

(Pause.)

SONYA. Just tell me: yes?

(YELENA nods.)

SEREBRYAKOV. *(to TELEGIN)* I've found that it's possible to make peace with bad health, that's the way things go sometimes, but what I *can't* stand is the way you people live here in the country. It's like I've fallen off the earth onto some strange planet!

Take a seat, ladies and gentleman, please.

Sonya!

(SONYA does not hear him. She stands, her head lowered, suffering.)

SEREBRYAKOV. Sonya!

(pause)

She's not listening.

(to MARINA)

You, Nanny, sit.

(MARINA sits and knits a stocking.)

SEREBRYAKOV. Ladies and gentlemen. Please hang your ears, as they say, on the nail of attention.

(He laughs.)

VOINITSKY. *(troubled)* I'm not needed. Can I go?

SEREBRYAKOV. No, no, you're needed here more than anyone else.

VOINITSKY. What do you want from me?

SEREBRYAKOV. You…why do you seem so angry?

(Pause.)

SEREBRYAKOV. If I am guilty before thee, Vanya, pardon me, please!

VOINITSKY. Oh stop it. Just tell us what this is about.

*(Enter **MARIA VASILYEVNA**.)*

SEREBRYAKOV. And here is *Maman.*

I will begin.

(Pause.)

SEREBRYAKOV. Hm. Well. "I have asked you all to come here, gentlemen, in order to tell you that a Government Inspector will be coming to visit us."

(a short pause)

All jokes aside, uh…I'm here to discuss something quite serious. I've gathered you all to ask for your help and advice. As you know, I'm a scholar, a, uh, absent-minded professor, and I've never been very good at the practical side of life. I've always needed the help of competent people like yourselves—Ivan Petrovich, of course, and you, Ilya Ilyich, and of course you, dear *Maman*…

Let's see. *Manet omnes una nox*…that is, we all walk under God. I am old, I am sick, and I think it's important that I settle my affairs inasmuch as and insofar as they concern my family. My life is almost over, so I'm not thinking of myself, but I have a young wife and an unmarried daughter.

(Pause.)

SEREBRYAKOV. To continue living in the country is impossible. It's become clear that we are...we are not made for this place. And you all know we can't live in the city just off the profits from the estate. If we were to sell, for example, the forest, that would get us a small sum of money but no annual salary. It's important, you see, that we seek out a continuous and more or less specified source of income. Omitting the details, let me propose to you the outline of a still very general idea. This estate yields an average rate of no greater than two percent. I propose that we sell it. If we convert the cash from the liquidation into interest-bearing securities, we'll receive between four and five percent, and if I'm correct I believe there would be a surplus of several thousand that would allow us to purchase a not-too-large dacha in Finland.

VOINITSKY. I'm sorry. Hold on.

I think I misheard you.

Please repeat what you just said.

SEREBRYAKOV. We would convert the money into interest bearing securities, and use the remaining surplus to buy a dacha in Finland.

VOINITSKY. No, no, not the Finland part. You said something else.

SEREBRYAKOV. I propose that we sell the estate.

VOINITSKY. That's it. Yes. You'll sell the estate. Excellent! That's a brilliant idea.

And where do you propose I go, along with my decrepit mother and Sonya here?

SEREBRYAKOV. All of this will be decided in time. Not right away.

VOINITSKY. I just realized something. Until now I've been operating under a false assumption. Until now I had some insane, nonsensical notion that this estate belongs to Sonya! Yes, my late father bought this place as a dowry for my sister. But I was naïve, I didn't know the law was *Turkish* to you, and so I thought that the estate was being passed down from my sister to her daughter, Sonya.

SEREBRYAKOV. Yes, this estate belongs to Sonya. Nobody's disputing that. Without Sonya's agreement, I wouldn't sell it. Although I do think this would be a wise move for her.

VOINITISKY. This is unfathomable. I can't...it's...it's unfathomable. Either I've lost my mind or...or...

MARIA VASILYEVNA. Jean, don't contradict him. Alexander knows better than us...he understands how these things work.

VOINITSKY. Someone give me water!

(He drinks some water.)

VOINITSKY. Say whatever you want. You can say whatever you want to me.

SEREBRYAKOV. I don't understand why you're getting so worked up. I'm not saying my idea is perfect. If everyone thinks it's unsuitable, I won't pursue it.

(Pause.)

TELEGIN. *(confused)* Your Excellency, I also have a, uh, reverence for academia and a family connection to it as well. It might interest you to know that my brother Gregori Ilyich's wife's brother—maybe you know him?—Konstantin Trofimovich Lakedemonov, held a master's degree, and he—

VOINITSKY. Hold on, Waffles, we're talking about something.

(to **SEREBRYAKOV***)*

Actually, you know what? You should ask *him*. This estate was bought from his uncle.

SEREBRYAKOV. Akh, what do you want me to ask him? What's the point?

VOINITSKY. This estate was bought for what was in those days the equivalent of ninety-five thousand. Father paid seventy thousand and a debt of twenty-five thousand remained. Now listen to me: my father would have never bought this estate if I hadn't refused my entire inheritance for the benefit of my sister, whom I loved with my entire being. What's more, I worked here for decades, I worked *like an ox,* and I'm the one who paid off the debt.

SEREBRYAKOV. I regret starting this conversation.

VOINITSKY. This estate is free of debt and this house is still standing because of me, because of the work that I've put into it. And now that I'm old, you're going to drag me out by the neck!

SEREBRYAKOV. I don't understand why you're so worked up about this! I merely—

VOINITSKY. For twenty-five years I've managed this entire estate, I've worked, I've sent you money, I've been your groveling little bookkeeper and not once in twenty-five years, not once did you stop and thank me. All this time—starting when I was a very young man and up until now—I have received the same salary from you, five hundred rubles a year—a *beggar* makes more than that—and not once, not once, has it occurred to you to raise my salary by a single ruble!

SEREBRYAKOV. But Ivan Petrovich, how could I have known? I'm not a practical person, I don't understand these things…You could have given yourself a raise, however much you wanted.

VOINITSKY. Why didn't I steal? Is that what you're asking? You're holding me in contempt because I didn't steal? *That* was the right thing to do?

MARIA VASILYEVNA. *(sternly)* Jean!

TELEGIN. *(worried)* Vanya, don't do this…please don't do this…I'm shaking…

Why ruin a good friendship?

(kisses him)

Don't do this.

VOINITSKY. For twenty-five years I've lived here with my mother, huddled in these four walls like a...

All our thoughts and feelings belonged to you. We spent days talking about your work, bragging to people about you, we spoke your name like you were some kind of saint...I spent nights reading idiotic academic journals and books...all of which I now deeply despise!

TELEGIN. Don't do this, Vanya...please don't do this...I can't...

SEREBRYAKOV. *(angry)* What do you want from me?

VOINITSKY. You were above us...you were the embodiment of some kind of supreme order...we could recite your essays by heart...

And now my eyes have been opened! I see everything! You write about art, and you understand nothing about art! All of your writing, all of those essays, they aren't worth a half-kopeck! So congratulations! You fooled everyone!

SEREBRYAKOV. Ladies and gentleman. Will someone please calm him down? I'm leaving.

YELENA. Ivan Petrovich, you have to stop talking! Do you hear me?

VOINITISKY. I will *not* stop talking!

*(blocking **SEREBRYAKOV**'s way)*

I'm not finished! You ruined my life! I haven't lived! I never lived! Thanks to you I destroyed the best years of my life!

You are my...my...my worst enemy!

YELENA. I'm leaving. This is hell.

(screaming)

I CAN'T TAKE IT ANYMORE!

VOINITSKY. My life is over.

I'm talented, I'm smart…If I'd had a normal adulthood
I could've been a Schopenhauer or a Dostoyevsky…
Oh God. I'm going crazy. I'm losing my mind. Mother.
Mother. I'm in despair. Help me! Mother!

MARIA VASILYEVNA. *(sternly)* You have to listen to Alexandre!

*(**SONYA** gets down on her knees before **MARINA** and
holds on to her for dear life.)*

SONYA. Nannechka. Nannechka.

VOINITSKY. Mother! Help me! What do I do? No, don't tell
me, don't tell me. I know what I need to do.

*(to **SEREBRYAKOV**)*

You're going to remember me!

*(He exits through the center door. **MARIA** goes after him.)*

SEREBRYAKOV. Ladies and gentleman, I, I…just please
keep that lunatic away from me. I can't live under one
roof with him anymore. He lives there…

(indicating center door)

…right beside me…he has to move into town. Or to
another part of the house. Or I'll move out. But I can't
stay in this house with him.

YELENA. *(to her husband)* We're leaving today. We have to
leave today.

SEREBRYAKOV. He's a nonentity.

He's a nonentity.

*(**SONYA**, still on her knees, turns to her father, and
nervously, through tears:)*

SONYA. Please be kind to him, Papa. Uncle Vanya and I are
so unhappy!

(holding back despair)

Please…have a little mercy. Remember, when you were
younger, Uncle Vanya and Babushka would stay up all
night translating books for you, and they'd copy out
your papers…they'd be up all night long! Uncle Vanya
and I never took a day off, we were always afraid to

spend a kopeck on ourselves because we wanted to send everything to you...he's a good man, Papa! I'm not saying this well, but I...you have to understand what we've been through. Have a little mercy!

YELENA. *(distressed, to her husband)* For god's sake, Alexander, go and reason with him.

SEREBRYAKOV. Fine, fine, I'll try to reason with him...I'm not blaming him for anything...I'm not even that angry...but you have to agree that he's behaving inappropriately.

I'll go find him.

(He exits through the center door.)

YELENA. Be gentle with him...try to calm him down...

(She exits behind him.)

SONYA. *(pressing herself to* **MARINA***)* Nannechka! Nannechka!

MARINA. It's nothing, little girl. The ganders squawk and then stop...Squawk and then stop...

SONYA. Nannechka!

MARINA. *(stroking her head)* You're shaking, like you've been out in the cold. Now, now, my little orphan, God is merciful. Some linden tea, maybe some raspberry, and this will pass too...don't cry, little orphan-girl...

(looking towards the center door, finally getting angry)

Those ganders need to take a rest.

Sometimes I wish they'd all fall in a hole!

(A shot rings out offstage; **YELENA** *screams;* **SONYA** *flinches.)*

MARINA. What are they—

*(***SEREBRYAKOV** *runs in, reeling from shock.)*

SEREBRYAKOV. Stop him! Someone hold him back! He's lost his mind!

*(***YELENA** *and* **VOINITSKY** *struggle in the doorway.)*

YELENA. *(attempting to take his revolver away)* Give it to me! Goddammit, give it to me!

VOINITSKY. Let go, Hélène! Let me go!

(He frees himself, then looks around for **SEREBRYAKOV.***)*

VOINITSKY. Where is he?

(He shoots at **SEREBRYAKOV.***)*

VOINITSKY. Bang!

(Pause.)

VOINITSKY. Did I hit him?

(pause)

I missed again?!

(angry)

Aw, go to hell...

You can all just go to hell.

(He drops the revolver and, totally exhausted, sits in a chair.)

*(***SEREBRYAKOV*** is stunned.* **YELENA** *leans against the wall, faint.)*

YELENA. Take me away from here. Take me away, kill me...I just...

I can't stay here another minute.

VOINITSKY. *(in despair)* What am I doing?

SONYA. *(quietly)* Nannechka! Nannechka!

(Curtain.)

ACT FOUR

(**IVAN PETROVICH**'s room; this is his bedroom and also the office for the estate. There is a large table at the window covered with his accounting books and all sorts of papers, a writing desk, a cabinet, and scales. A smaller table for **ASTROV**. On this table are materials for drawing; paints, and a portfolio.)

(A cage with a starling.)

(On the wall, for no reason, a map of Africa.)

(An enormous stiff cotton sofa.)

(To the left, a door, leading to another suite of rooms; to the right, a door to the vestibule. Beside the door on the right there is a long narrow carpet so the peasants don't drag dirt in.)

(It's an autumn evening. Quiet.)

(**TELEGIN** and **MARINA** sit facing each other, winding wool for knitting.)

TELEGIN. Hurry up, Marina Timofeyevna. They're about to say goodbye.

MARINA. (trying to wind faster) There's not much left.

TELEGIN. They're leaving for Kharkov.

They're going to live there.

MARINA. Mm-hm.

It's for the best.

TELEGIN. They got scared. "I won't stay here another hour!" said Yelena Andreyevna. "We're leaving! We have to go!" "We'll live in Kharkov," she said, "We'll find a place and then send for our things…"

So they're traveling light.

I guess it's not their destiny to live here.

God's will.

MARINA. It's for the best. They've been stirring things up... and that shooting...! It was disgraceful.

TELEGIN. Yes! It was a scene worthy of Aivazovsky!

MARINA. To witness such a thing. At my age.

(Pause.)

MARINA. We'll go back to living the way we did before. Morning tea before eight, lunch before one, and in the evenings we'll sit down to a nice supper, the way people do everywhere. The Christian way.

(sighing)

It's been such a long time since I've tasted noodles.

TELEGIN. Oh yes.

This house has not seen noodles in a very long time.

(Pause.)

TELEGIN. ...A very long time.

(Pause.)

TELEGIN. You know what happened this morning, Marina Timofeyevna? I was walking through town and this shopkeeper came running after me and shouted: "HEY YOU! MOOCHER!"

It hurt my feelings.

MARINA. Oh, don't pay any attention to him, sweetie. We're all God's moochers.

(short pause)

You, me, Sonya, Ivan Petrovich...we know how to work hard, and we all contribute in our way.

Where is Sonya?

TELEGIN. In the garden. She's with the doctor, looking for Ivan Petrovich.

They're afraid he might hurt himself.

MARINA. Oh dear. Where is that gun?

TELEGIN. *(whispering)* I hid it in the basement!

MARINA. *(with a grin)* Bad boy!

(VOINITSKY and ASTROV enter from the yard.)

VOINITSKY. Leave me alone.

(to MARINA and TELEGIN)

You too…both of you…

Everyone go away! Just give me an hour by myself!

I can't stand you all watching me like this.

TELEGIN. Of course, Vanya.

Right away.

(He tiptoes away.)

MARINA. Oh, you're such an old gander!

(honking at him)

Wah-wah-wah!

(She gathers up her wool and leaves.)

VOINITSKY. *(to ASTROV)* You! Go away!

ASTROV. I'd be glad to, I've actually needed to leave for a while, but I repeat: I am not going until you return what you took from me.

VOINITSKY. I didn't take anything from you.

ASTROV. I'm serious. Don't make me follow you around. I need to get out of here.

VANYA. I said I didn't take anything.

(They both sit down.)

ASTROV. Fine. Then I'll stay a little longer. But eventually I'm going to use force. I'll tie you up and search you, Vanya. I'm absolutely serious.

VOINITSKY. Whatever you want.

(Pause.)

VOINITSKY. I looked like an idiot. To shoot at someone—twice—and not hit him!

I'll never forgive myself.

ASTROV. If you didn't want to miss, you should've aimed at your own forehead.

*(**VOINITSKY** shrugs.)*

VOINITSKY. It's so strange. I've attempted murder, but no one is arresting me and no one is taking me to court.

You know what? That means they all just think I'm crazy.

(laughing bitterly)

I'm a madman.

Yes, I'm a madman, but the people who listen to the Professor, that old…that old magician, the people who deny his lack of talent and his stupidity and…his…his…his *heartlessness,* those people are aren't mad at all. People who marry old men and then lie to them in front of everyone…no no! Those people are perfectly sane! I saw. I saw you kiss her.

ASTROV. All right. Fine.

I kissed her.

And you know what I have to say to you about it?

*(**ASTROV** puts his thumb to his nose and wiggles his fingers.)*

VOINITSKY. *(glancing at the door)* It's a terrible, terrible world that lets people like you get away with things.

ASTROV. All right, stop. This is stupid.

VOINITSKY. Why? I'm a madman. I'm not responsible. I have the right to talk nonsense.

ASTROV. The joke is getting old. You're not a madman, you're a fool and you're a creep.

You know, I used to think that being a creep meant you were sick or abnormal, but lately I've come to the conclusion that we're all creeps. Everyone in the world, behaving naturally, is a complete creep.

So the truth is, Vanya, you're totally normal.

VOINITSKY. *(covering his face with his hands)* I'm so ashamed.

If you only knew how ashamed I am.

It's this sharp...it's this very acute feeling of shame and it's worse than any physical pain.

(with great melancholy)

It's unbearable.

(He leans over the table.)

VOINITSKY. What do I do. What do I do.

ASTROV. Nothing.

VOINITSKY. Give me something for the pain!

Oh god. I'm forty-seven. Let's say I live to be sixty. I still have thirteen years left. That's so long. How do I... how am I going to live for thirteen more years? How will I fill my days? You have to understand...

*(fitfully pressing **ASTROV**'s hand)*

...please understand, if I could just start over again. If I could wake up on a clear, quiet morning and know that something new is beginning, that the past has been forgotten...that it drifted away like smoke...

To begin a new life.

Please tell me.

How do I begin?

Where do I begin?

ASTROV. *(annoyed)* All right, all right. Look, there is no other new life out there.

We have the same predicament. It's hopeless.

VOINITSKY. ...It is?

ASTROV. I'm convinced of this.

VOINITSKY. Please give me something…

(he touches his heart)

It's burning…I'm telling you…it's burning up…

ASTROV. Stop it!

(He softens.)

ASTROV. Look, in one hundred, two hundred years there will be people who look back and laugh at us because we lived our lives so foolishly and tastelessly. Maybe those people will have found a way to be happy. But us…

You and I have only one hope left. The hope that when we're finally laid to rest in our graves, the visions that greet us will not be unpleasant.

(sighing)

Listen, brother. In this entire district there were only two respectable, intelligent people: you and me. But in ten years this way of living has dragged us both down; it's poisoned our blood, and we've become vulgar, just like everyone else.

(more animated)

But this is all a distraction, isn't it? You need to give back what you took from me.

VOINITSKY. I didn't take anything from you.

ASTROV. You took a vial of morphine out of my bag.

(Pause.)

ASTROV. Listen. If you really want to end your life, walk into the forest and shoot yourself in the head. But give me back my morphine, or else there'll be talk and they'll think I gave it to you. It'll be enough having to perform your autopsy. You think that's going to be fun for me?

*(**SONYA** enters.)*

VOINITSKY. Leave me alone.

ASTROV. *(to* SONYA*)* Sophia Alexandrovna, your uncle has taken a vial of my morphine and he won't give it back. Tell him that this is stupid. And I don't have time for it. I have to go.

SONYA. Uncle Vanya, did you take that vial of morphine?

(Pause.)

ASTROV. He took it. I'm positive.

SONYA. Give it back.

Why are you doing this to us?

(gently)

Give it back, Uncle Vanya!

I'm probably just as unhappy as you are, but I'm not giving in to despair. I...I endure my unhappiness and I will endure it until my life comes to its natural end.

You have to endure it too.

(Pause.)

SONYA. Give it back!

(kisses his hands)

Dear sweet, decent Uncle Vanya, give it back!

(weeping)

You're a good man. Take pity on all of us and give it back.

You can endure the pain, Uncle Vanya! Endure it!

*(*VOINITSKY *finally retrieves the vial of morphine from his desk and returns it to* ASTROV.*)*

VOINITSKY. Here. Take it.

(to SONYA*)*

But we have to start working again. Now. We have to do something. Otherwise I can't...I can't...

SONYA. Yes, yes. Of course. Right after we see them off, we'll sit down to work.

(She nervously arranges pages on the table.)

SONYA. We've let everything go.

(ASTROV puts the vial back into his doctor's bag and tightens the strap.)

ASTROV. I'll be on my way.

(YELENA ANDREYEVNA enters.)

YELENA. Ivan Petrovich, are you here? We're leaving.

Go find Alexander, he wants to tell you something.

SONYA. Come on, Uncle Vanya.

(taking VOINITSKY by the arm)

Let's go.

You and Papa need to make up.

It's important.

(SONYA and VOINITSKY exit.)

YELENA. I'm leaving.

(She gives ASTROV her hand.)

YELENA. Say goodbye.

ASTROV. Already.

YELENA. The horses are waiting.

ASTROV. ...Goodbye.

YELENA. You promised me that you'd leave today.

ASTROV. I remember. I'm going to.

(Pause.)

ASTROV. You're afraid.

(taking her hand)

Is it really that frightening?

YELENA. Yes.

ASTROV. That means you've thought about staying.

Well?

Look, tomorrow, come to the forest...

YELENA. No. It's been already been decided. That's why I can look you in the eyes right now...I know I'm leaving.

But I want...let me ask you for one thing?

Think better of me.

I want you to respect me.

ASTROV. Akh! Just...

(making a gesture of impatience)

Just stay.

I'm asking you to stay.

Admit that there's nothing productive left for you to do in this world. Admit that your entire life has been unremarkable and you're bored and sooner or later you're going to give in to your feelings anyway. I'm telling you, it's unavoidable. And it shouldn't happen somewhere in Kharkov or Kursk. it should happen right here. In the open air. It's autumn, it's beautiful; it would be poetic. There's a forest, there are lots of dilapidated Turgenev mansions...

YELENA. You're funny.

I'm angry at you, but still...I will always remember you with pleasure.

You're an interesting, original person. And since we're never going to see each other again, I'm not going to lie. I was captivated by you.

Well. Let's shake hands and part as friends.

Think good thoughts about me.

ASTROV. *(pressing her hand)* All right. Go.

(thoughtfully)

You know, it's not that you're a bad person. You seem to be sincere enough; there's just something deeply strange about you. You came here with your husband and everyone had to drop their work to spend the summer taking care of you. You both infected all of us with your *uselessness.* I was infatuated, I did nothing for an entire month. People got sick and the peasants used my new forest to graze their livestock. Wherever you and your husband go, you bring destruction...I'm joking of course, but still...it's very strange.

Now that I'm thinking about it, if you'd stayed, the devastation would have been enormous. It would have been the end of me.

And you would have gotten in a lot of trouble.

So. Go.

Finita la commedia!

(YELENA takes a pencil from his desk and puts it in her pocket.)

YELENA. I'm taking your pencil.

ASTROV. God, it's so strange. We got to know each other, and now we're never going to see each other again.

That's how the world works, I guess.

Look, no one is here, before Uncle Vanya walks in with his flowers, let me kiss you. A goodbye kiss. Yes?

(He kisses her on the cheek.)

ASTROV. Well. All right. That was very nice.

YELENA. I wish you the best.

(She looks around.)

YELENA. Oh god. Here goes. For once in my life!

(She embraces him fully, impulsively, and then they both immediately walk away from each other.)

YELENA. I need to go.

ASTROV. Then please, go quickly.

If the horses are ready, go.

YELENA. Someone's coming.

(They listen.)

ASTROV. *(softly)* Finita!

(Enter SEREBRYAKOV, VOINITSKY, MARIA VASILYEVNA *[with a book],* TELEGIN *and* SONYA.*)*

SEREBRYAKOV. "He who dwells in the past shall have his eye plucked out." I've had so many strange experiences and reconsidered so many things in the past few hours that I now feel equipped to write an entire treatise on how to live. For the benefit of future generations.

I accept your apology and I leave asking for your forgiveness.

Goodbye.

(He kisses VOINITSKY *three times.)*

VOINITSKY. You'll be receiving the same amount you received before, every month, on time. Everything will go back to the way it was.

*(*YELENA ANDREYEVNA *embraces* SONYA.*)*

SEREBRYAKOV. *(kissing* MARIA VASILYEVNA*'s hands) Maman…*

MARIA VASILYEVNA. *(kissing him)* Alexandre, have someone take your picture and then send me the photograph. You are so precious to me.

TELEGIN. Farewell, Your Excellency! Do not forget us!

SEREBRYAKOV. *(kisses his daughter)* Goodbye.

Goodbye, everyone!

(giving his hand to ASTROV*)*

Thank you for the excellent company. I respect your, uh, way of thinking and your enthusiasm and spontaneity. But allow an old man some parting words—just one observation—

(to all)

Do something with your lives, ladies and gentleman!

You must always take action and *do* something!

(he bows to everyone)

I wish you all the best!

(He exits. **MARIA VASILYEVNA** *and* **SONYA** *walk behind him.)*

VOINITSKY. *(earnestly kissing the hand of* YELENA ANDREYEVNA*)* Goodbye.

Forgive me.

We will never see each other again.

YELENA. *(touched)* Goodbye, sweet man.

(She kisses him on the head and exits.)

ASTROV. *(to* **TELEGIN***)* Hey Waffles. Tell them to get my horses ready.

TELEGIN. I hear you loud and clear, my friend.

(He exits.)

(Only **ASTROV** *and* **VOINITSKY** *are left.)*

*(***ASTROV*** starts removing his paints from the table and putting them in his suitcase.)*

ASTROV. Why don't you see them off?

VOINITSKY. They can go, but I…I can't.

This is too difficult.

I need to occupy myself.

Work, work…

(He riffles through the pages on the table.)

(Pause. The ringing of harness bells can be heard.)

ASTROV. They're gone.

Don't worry, the professor is happy.

And he'll never come back. Not for anything in the world.

*(***MARINA*** enters.)*

MARINA. They're gone.

(She sits down in an armchair and starts to knit a stocking. **SONYA** *enters.)*

SONYA. They're gone.

> *(she wipes her eyes)*

> God willing they'll arrive safely.

> *(to* VOINITSKY*)*

> Well, Uncle Vanya?

> Let's do something.

VOINITSKY. Work, work…

SONYA. It's been a long, long time since we've sat together at this table.

> *(She lights the lamp on the table.)*

SONYA. There's no ink…

> *(She takes the inkwell, walks over to the cabinet, and fills it with ink.)*

SONYA. I'm sad they're gone.

> *(*MARIA *enters slowly.)*

MARIA. They're gone!

> *(She sits down and plunges herself into a book.)*

> *(*SONYA *sits at the table and flips through the accounting ledger.)*

SONYA. All right, Uncle Vanya. Let's do the accounts before anything else. We let everything go. They sent for them again today. You do one account, I'll do another.

VOINITSKY. *(writing, talking to himself)* "Account number… Mr…"

> *(They both write silently.)*

MARINA. *(yawning)* Time for beddy-bye.

ASTROV. It's quiet now. Just the scratching of your pens. A cricket chirping.

> It's so warm and cozy…I don't want to leave.

> *(His harness bells are heard.)*

ASTROV. My horses are almost ready.

All that's left is goodbye.

Goodbye to you, my friends, and goodbye to my little table...off we go.

(He puts his maps into a portfolio.)

MARINA. What's the big hurry? Sit with us for a while.

ASTROV. I can't.

VOINITSKY. *(writing)* "And from the debt remaining we have two seventy-five..."

(The **HIRED MAN** *enters.)*

HIRED MAN. Your horses are waiting, Mikhail Lvovich.

ASTROV. Yes, I heard.

(He hands him his doctor's bag, his suitcase and his portfolio.)

ASTROV. Here, take these. Be careful not to bend the portfolio.

HIRED MAN. Of course.

(He leaves.)

ASTROV. Well...

(He goes to say goodbye.)

SONYA. When will we see you again?

ASTROV. Ah...probably not before the summer. Winter is... unlikely.

If anything happens, if you need anything, just let me know—I'll come.

(pressing her hand)

Thank you for the food and the hospitality and for your...your kindness...

(they look at each other)

Thanks for everything, I guess.

(He walks over to **MARINA** *and kisses her head.)*

ASTROV. Goodbye, old dear.

MARINA. Just like that you're leaving without having tea.

ASTROV. I don't want any, Nanny.

MARINA. Maybe a teeny weeny drop of vodka?

ASTROV. *(hesitating)* Maybe…

(**MARINA** *exits.*)

ASTROV. My horse is limping for some reason. I noticed yesterday when Petrushka went to walk it.

VOINITSKY. Have it reshoed.

ASTROV. I'll have to go to the blacksmith in Rozhdestveno. Akh, there's no avoiding it.

(**ASTROV** *walks over to the map of Africa and looks at it.*)

ASTROV. It must be very hot in Africa right now.

VOINITSKY. Mm-hm.

Probably.

(**MARINA** *returns with a tray, on it glass of vodka and a piece of bread.*)

MARINA. Drink up.

(**ASTROV** *drinks the vodka.*)

MARINA. To your health, sweetie-pie.

(She bows deep.)

MARINA. Have a little bread with it.

ASTROV. No, I'll have it like this.

All right.

Goodbye!

(to **MARINA***)*

Don't see me off, Nanny. It isn't necessary.

(*He leaves;* **SONYA** *follows him with a candle to see him off.* **MARINA** *sits down in her armchair.*)

VOINITSKY. *(writing)* February second, vegetable oil, twenty pounds. February sixteenth, vegetable oil, twenty pounds…Buckwheat kasha…

(Harness bells are heard.)

MARINA. He's gone.

(Pause.)

*(**SONYA** returns and places the candle on the table.)*

SONYA. He's gone…

VOINITSKY. *(adding it up on his accounting form and noting it)* Altogether…we have fifteen…twenty-five…

*(**SONYA** sits down and starts writing again.)*

MARINA. *(yawning)* We're all sinners…every one of us…

*(**TELEGIN** comes in on tiptoe, sits by the door and quietly tunes his guitar.)*

VOINITSKY. *(to **SONYA**, running his hand over her hair)* It's so difficult for me.

If you only knew how difficult it is!

SONYA. What can we do?

We have to live.

(Pause.)

SONYA. We'll live, Uncle Vanya.

We'll live through a long, long row of days and drawn-out evenings; we'll endure the trials that fate sends us; we'll work for others; and finally in our old age, having never known peace, when our hour comes, we'll die. And from beyond the grave we'll be able to look back and say that we suffered, that we wept, that we were bitter, and God will take pity on us, and you and I, Uncle, dear Uncle, we'll see a radiant new life, beautiful, full of grace, and we'll smile and look back tenderly at our past unhappiness.

And we'll rest. I believe this, Uncle, I believe in it passionately.

(She gets before him on her knees and lays her head in his hands; in a weary voice:)

We'll rest!

(TELEGIN *starts playing chords on the guitar.)*

SONYA. We'll rest! We'll hear the angels, we'll see the entire sky lit up in diamonds, we'll watch all of our suffering drown in a divine mercy that fills up the world. Everything will be quiet and gentle and tender and sweet. I believe that. I really do.

(She wipes his tears with a handkerchief.)

Poor, poor Uncle Vanya, you're crying…

(through tears)

You've never known happiness, but hold on.

We'll rest…

(she embraces him)

We'll rest!

(The watchman knocks about outside.)

(TELEGIN *plays a song on the guitar.* **MARIA** *writes in the margins of her pages;* **MARINA** *knits a stocking.)*

SONYA. We'll rest.

End of Play.

PRONUNCIATION GUIDE

SyeryebryaKOV (luckily no one ever says this out loud)

Ivan PeTROVich

Sophia AlekSANDrovna

Yelena AnDREyevna

TyelYEgin (hard g)

Mikhail LVOvich

Marina TimoFEYevna

Maria VaSEElyevna

ILya ILyich (EELya EElich)

Pavel AlekSEYyevich

Vera PeTROVna

MAH-leetskoye

BA-tyoosh-kov

KonstantEEN TroFEEmovich LakyedyeMONov

AivaZOVsky

LYEN-ochka

SON-yechka

NAN-yechka

ТЫ: this is the informal "you." It's a sign of familiarity. It sounds a little like "toy" but with a lot of "ee" in the vowel, a combo of the sounds "oy" and "ee." It works if you try saying "ee" with your mouth in the "oy" position."